Don't

Written by Jill Eggleton

In this cabinet
there are bottles.
On the bottles
there are words.
On some of the bottles
there is a word,
poison!
Don't touch!

poison

In this shed there are bottles and cans.

The word **poison** is on some of the bottles and cans, too.
Don't touch!

5

Look at this frog.
You can't see the word poison on it.
But this frog has poison in its skin.
Don't touch this frog!

skin

frog

7

Look at the fangs
on this snake.
These fangs have poison
in them.
This animal is
very dangerous.
If you see one,
don't touch!

fang

snake

9

Here is a caterpillar.
Look at the hair
on its back.
But look out!

The hair has **poison** in it.
If you see a caterpillar
like this, don't touch!

hair

caterpillar

11

Some things have words
that say **poison**!
Some animals have poison
in their skin,
in their fangs, and
in their hair!

13

These things
are dangerous.
Don't touch!

Index

things that can be
poisonous

Guide Notes

Title: Don't Touch
Stage: Early (4) – Green

Genre: Nonfiction (Expository)
Approach: Guided Reading
Processes: Thinking Critically, Exploring Language, Processing Information
Written and Visual Focus: Photographs (static images), Labels, Index

THINKING CRITICALLY
(sample questions)
- Tell the children this book is about things that we don't touch because they are poisonous.
- Look at the title and read it to the children.
- Focus the children's attention on the Index. Ask: "What are you going to find out about in this book?"
- If you want to find out about a poisonous frog, on which page would you look?
- If you want to find out about a poisonous snake, on which page would you look?
- What do you think might happen if you touch things that are poisonous?

EXPLORING LANGUAGE

Terminology
Title, cover, photographs, author, photographers

Vocabulary
Interest words: cabinet, bottles, poison, touch, shed, dangerous, caterpillar
High-frequency word: their, these
Positional word: on
Contraction: don't

Print Conventions
Capital letter for sentence beginnings, periods, commas, exclamation mark